HYLAS

Hylas Publishing

First Published in 2005 by Hylas Publishing
129 Main Street, Irvington, New York, 10533

Publisher: Sean Moore
Creative Director: Karen Prince
Book Design: Miles Parsons and Pat Covert
Produced by: Cliff Road Books

First American Edition published in 2005
02 03 04 05 10 9 8 7 6 5 4 3 2 1

ISBN: 1-59258-101-3

Photography by Keith Harrelson
Costumes by Janet Tatum

Grateful acknowledgment is made to Margaret Jones Davis and staff at
Creative Dog Training in Birmingham, Alabama, without whom this
book would not have been possible, and especially to (in order of
appearance): Eeyore Davis, Oatmeal Davis, Scutter Buck Carlson,
Zelda McGowin, Brutus Kennedy, Darby Austin, Annie Glenn, Sophie
Windham, Simon Sullivan, Spike Stanfa, Maggie Austin, Bandit Powell,
Truman Sullivan, and Gus Moffett.

Printed and bound in Italy
Distributed by National Book Network

www.hylaspublishing.com

SNOW WHITE
AND THE
SEVEN DWARFS

HYLAS

$\mathcal{O}$nce upon a time a queen was sewing. She pricked her finger with the needle and, as drops of red blood fell on the snowy linen, she thought, "If only I had a daughter as pretty as a red rose in the snow."

Before long the queen did have a daughter. She was as beautiful as a red rose in the snow. The queen named her Snow White.

Sadly, the queen died while Snow White was still a baby. The King married again. The new queen was beautiful but very selfish and vain. She could even be cruel. No one in the palace liked her.

Every morning when she got up, and every evening before she went to bed, the queen stood before the magic mirror on her wall and said, "Mirror mirror on the wall, who is the fairest one of all?" And the magic mirror always said: "You are the fairest one of all."

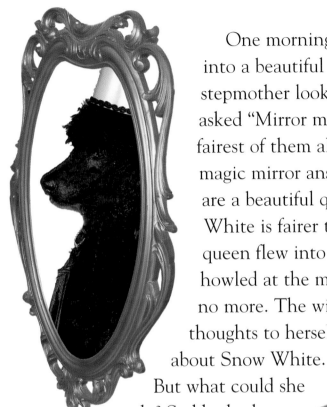

One morning, after Snow White had grown into a beautiful young woman, the wicked stepmother looked into the mirror as usual and asked "Mirror mirror on the wall, who is the fairest of them all? And on this morning, the magic mirror answered: "I cannot tell a lie. You are a beautiful queen it is true. But Snow White is fairer than you." At this the wicked queen flew into a rage. "This cannot be!" She howled at the mirror. But the mirror would say no more. The wicked queen thought evil thoughts to herself. She must do something about Snow White. But what could she do? Suddenly the queen had an idea.

$\mathcal{S}$he told her
serving maid to go and
fetch the palace
huntsman. As she
waited for him to
arrive, her evil plan
took shape.

When the
huntsman arrived, the
evil queen said: "I want you
to take Snow White into the
woods and kill her. Don't
return to the palace without
proof that Snow White is
gone for good!

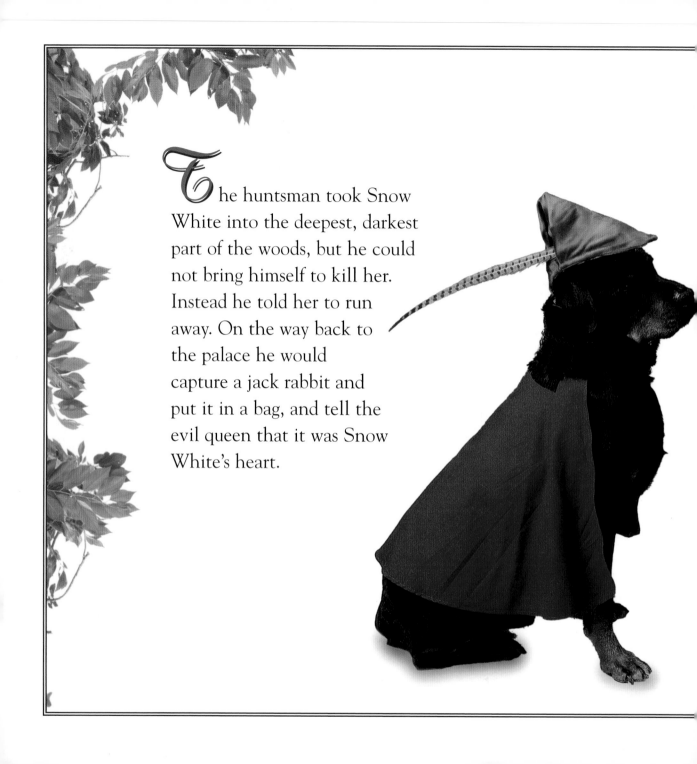

The huntsman took Snow White into the deepest, darkest part of the woods, but he could not bring himself to kill her. Instead he told her to run away. On the way back to the palace he would capture a jack rabbit and put it in a bag, and tell the evil queen that it was Snow White's heart.

Snow White made her way through the woods, tired and hungry. At last she came to a cottage. When no one answered the door she went inside. There she found a small table, with seven chairs and seven places set for supper. But Snow White was so tired, all she could think about was curling up and going to sleep, which she did.

That night the seven dwarfs came home to find Snow White sound asleep in their cottage. "Oh my! Look how beautiful she is!" they whispered. They gathered around the beautiful princess, being careful not to wake her.

In the morning, Snow White told the dwarfs how she came to the cottage. The dwarfs were kind and understanding. They told Snow White that if she would help with the cooking and cleaning, she could stay as long as she wanted. "But you must not open the door while we are at work. Don't let anyone in! The wicked queen will find you, and try to get you! So keep the door locked!"

The next morning when the evil queen looked in the mirror, she was furious to hear its words: "Oh queen you are beautiful it is true, but Snow White still lives, and is more beautiful than you." The mirror told the queen where Snow White was hiding. The queen, her heart black with malice, changed into shabby clothes, disguising herself as an old woman, and set out to find Snow White.

When the queen, in her disguise, arrived at the dwarf's cottage, she knocked on the door and told Snow White she had a delicious basket of apples for her, "a gift for my new neighbor." Snow White couldn't bring herself to turn away the harmless old woman with her gift of apples, so she opened the door, took the basket, and bit into one of the apples. The queen, of course, had poisoned them, and she scampered off howling with glee at the sight of Snow White sinking to the floor in a swoon.

When the dwarfs came home they found Snow White in a slumber as deep as death. Nothing would wake her. They wept to see their beloved Snow White under the spell of the evil queen. Although she appeared to be dead, they didn't have the heart to bury her. The dwarfs decided to place her on a bed of flowers, in a beautiful clearing in the forest.

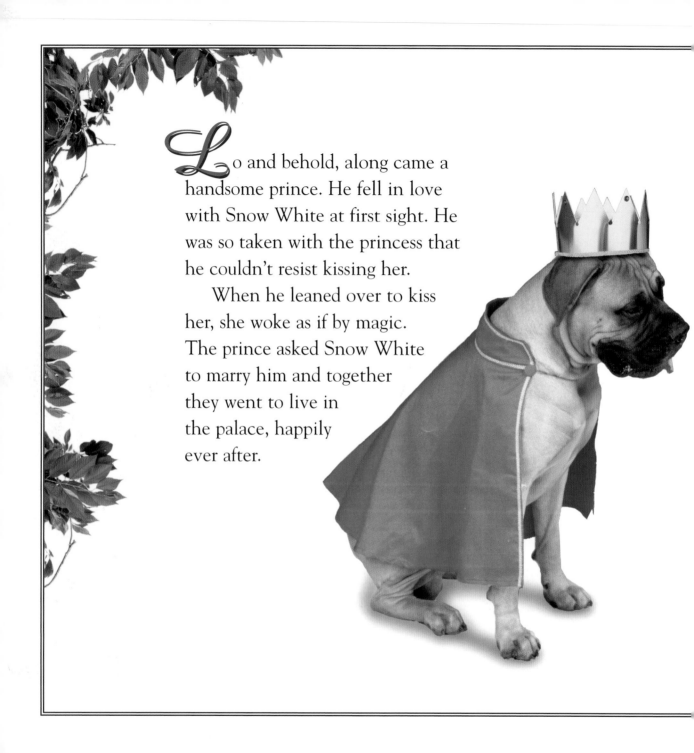

_L_o and behold, along came a
handsome prince. He fell in love
with Snow White at first sight. He
was so taken with the princess that
he couldn't resist kissing her.

When he leaned over to kiss
her, she woke as if by magic.
The prince asked Snow White
to marry him and together
they went to live in
the palace, happily
ever after.

When the magic mirror told the wicked queen about the marriage of Snow White and the prince, the queen tried to smash the mirror. But instead, she herself broke into a million pieces and dissolved like dust into the air, never to be seen again.